CW01180318

The Unexpurgated Diary of a Shanghai Baby

by
Elsie McCormick

With a Foreword by Graham Earnshaw

First Published in 1924

Reprinted by
China Economic Review Publishing
Hong Kong 2007

CER CLASSICS

The Unexpurgated Diary of a Shanghai Baby

By Elsie McCormick

With a foreword by Graham Earnshaw

ISBN-13: 978-988-99874-8-0

© 2007 China Economic Review Publishing

The Unexpurgated Diary of a Shanghai Baby was first published in 1924.
This edition with a new foreword is published by
China Economic Review Publishing,
Units C&D, 9/F Neich Tower,
128 Gloucester Road, Wanchai, Hong Kong

This book has been reset in 12pt Book Antigua. Spellings and punctuations are left as in the original edition.

All rights reserved. No part of this book may be reproduced in material form, by any means, whether graphic, electronic, mechanical or other, including photocopying or information storage, in whole or in part. May not be used to prepare other publications without written permission from the publisher.

CONTENTS

Foreword by Graham Earnshaw	vi
Chapter I	1
Chapter II	12
Chapter III	22
Chapter IV	32
Chapter V	40
Chapter VI	47
Chapter VII	55
Chapter VIII	65
ChapterIX	75
Chapter X	83
Chapter XI	94
Chapter XII	104
Epilogue	111
Glossary	113

FOREWORD
by Graham Earnshaw

THE WORLD of the Shanghailanders, the foreigner residents of Shanghai in the years up to the Japanese invasion of central China in 1937, and somewhat beyond, is no better illustrated than in this wonderful little book, the diary of a baby, aged perhaps around twelve months old. It was not actually written by the baby, at least I reluctantly assume that it was not, but rather by a lady named Elsie McCormick.

Ms McCormick was an American and in 1916, while studying at the University of California in Berkeley, she wrote out a list etiquette rules for female students wishing to live up to man's ideal of a perfect college woman, which included the following:

Rule 11. Do not study anything useful. Coeds should specialize in English and a diluted form of art history.

Rule 12. Always look and act as silly as

possible. If you can't think of anything else to do, giggle.

It was already clear that she was capable of producing delightful satirical barbs, a skill she was to make full use of in the *Unexpurgated Diary of a Shanghai Baby.*

In 1923, Elsie published a book called *Audacious Angles on China*, which sold well and included the first version of the *Unexpurgated Diary of a Shanghai baby.* A third edition of the Unexpurgated Diary was subsequently published as a stand-alone in Shanghai by the Chinese American Publishing Co in 1927. By the 1930s, Elsie was writing from the United States for the *New Yorker* magazine, which is all the confirmation that anyone needs of the quality of a writer's work.

What is depicted in this book is a foreigner family living in Shanghai in the 1920s. It was a city that was by then famous for being cosmopolitan and free-wheeling, where people lived hard, and either made a lot of money or crashed spectacularly.

Father works for a foreign company, and

clearly enjoys the nightlife entertainment opportunities provided by the city. Mother is freed from household chores, and even from looking after the baby, by the network of servants who run everything. The baby, meanwhile, sits on the floor and listens to the squabbles between his parents, while also enjoying another world – of which the American parents are blissfully unaware – of the Chinese maids and gardeners and drivers.

This idea of foreign children in Shanghai being brought up more by the servants than by the parents is well-documented, and old foreign residents who spent their younger years in the city often had experiences similar to those of the baby. J.G. Ballard, who wrote *Empire of the Sun* and other books about his experiences of growing up in Shanghai fifteen or twenty years after the baby in this book, is just one of many.

The foreigners in this Shanghailander world were spoiled rotten, of course. And this master/servant, Foreigner/Chinese culture, fueled by money on one side and poverty on the other, was created in Shanghai and transplanted after 1949 to Hong Kong. However, there appears to have been less fraternization between the Chinese servants and the children in Hong Kong than in the old Shanghai of the 1920s and 1930s.

The foreigners used to complain at their dinner parties about the servants, but it was the servants who actually kept the life of their households moving. A lot of the gentle jokes in the book involve the baby observing things the servants are doing which would appall the parents if they only knew. Like the room boy stealing the socks and the amah taking the baby to have an afternoon nap "with Chinese baby getting over mumps".

Shanghai in the 1920s was entering a phenomenal growth spurt, and there was a big influx of foreigners of all nationalities, white nationalities anyway, to take advantage of the opportunities. Most of the central city was built in those years. The mansions for the foreigners and rich Chinese and the vast swathes of two-storey jerry-built alleyway tenements, now being torn down to make way for the Shanghai of the 21st century, to house the hundreds of thousands of workers pouring in from the countryside to work in factories owned by people like the baby's father.

The foreigners spent their time at home or the club, where they could sign for everything. Cash did not change hands. They went to afternoon tea dances at the Palace Hotel or the Astor. They attended race meets at the race track which is now the People's Park in the center of the city. They got drunk a lot.

There are some references in the book which need to be explained.

On the first page, the baby refers to Opal Whitely and Daisy Ashford, names that mean nothing to us today but would have been instantly recognizable to Elsie's readers in the 1920s. Opal Whitely was a woman who published a book in 1920 called *Opal, the Journal of an Understanding Heart*, which she claimed was her diary written when she was a child, growing up in Oregon. It was a best-seller for a time, and then Opal was accused of making it up, and she spent most of the rest of her life in a mental institution in England.

Daisy Ashford, meanwhile, was an English writer who published a book in 1919 called *The Young Visiters*. She had written it at the age of nine, and it took digs at upper-class English society in the late 19th century. It was a big success, and remains in print today.

The baby and Elsie were obviously inspired by these two books by young writers, and decided to go one better.

We never find out the name of the baby, but it is male. We also know that the baby takes a definite dislike to a Japanese baby he meets in Hongkew Park. This piece of geographical information is useful because it indicates where the family was living – in the Hongkou district north of the Bund, beyond the Garden Bridge over the Soochow Creek, in what had once been the American Settlement.

The baby conducts his own little war against the Japanese baby, which is not *precisely* how the baby refers to its rival, reflecting the geopolitical situation of the times. Japan was on the rise through the 1920s and 1930s, leading in the end of the horrors of the China and Pacific theaters of the Second World War. Even in the early 1920s, westerners were mostly uncomfortable with this aggressive, militaristic and focused Oriental power, a sharp contrast to the messy, lovable and totally unfocused world of China where westerners seemed to feel very much at home.

Many of the foreigners of old Shanghai used to communicate with the swirling mass of Chinese people around them with pidgin English, a quite ridiculous mish-mash of words in which chop-chop meant "hurry" and "Ningbo more far" meant "a long way away". Carl Crow, the pioneer of the advertising industry in China in those years and author of *Foreign Devils in the Flowery Kingdom*, actually wrote some children's books in the dialect. He would have known Elsie McCormick for sure. Elsie thoughtfully provided a glossary of pidgin terms used in the book at the end.

Towards the end of the first chapter, one of the Chinese servants playing his *erhu* in the basement of the family's house inspires a reference to Mischa Elman, who was a very famous classical violinist who had just moved from Germany to the United States when this book was first published in 1923.

In Chapter Three, there is a reference to Jack Dempsey, a boxing champion and a sports superstar of his day, and a few chapters on to another famous boxer of the day, Jess Willard.

The roads of old Shanghai mostly had foreign names. Today's Huaihai Lu was Avenue Joffre, the main thoroughfare through the French Concession. Edinburgh Rd is now called Jiangsu Lu. Dongdaming Lu, in the area of Hongkou in which the family lived, was then called Broadway for a portion of its length and Seward Road beyond. Nanjing Rd West, as it is today, was then called Bubbling Well. Dixwell Rd, which gets a mention in Chapter 3, was another important road in the Hongkou area; it is today called Liyang Lu. Jessfield Park, where there was once a small zoo, is now called Zhongshan Park.

In Chapter 4, there is a reference to *the Empress of Asia*, one of the great passenger liners of that age, owned by Canadian Pacific Steamships Ltd and launched in 1912. The ship transported British troops to Shanghai in 1937 to bolster the garrison of the International Settlement and was finally sunk by the Japanese near Singapore in February 1942.

This book is all about a world that has gone. But the feeling of that golden world of the Shanghailanders between the two great wars of the 20th century is here to be savored.

Graham Earnshaw
Shanghai
December 2007

Chapter I

In Which the Baby Decides that "Home, Sweet Home" Must Have Been Written by Orphan . . . The Charms of Calling Sinza Road . . . Amah Stages a Funeral . . . The Strange Vagaries of Silk Host in Shanghai.

March 29

The family has been raving about somebody called Opal Whitely and somebody else called Daisy Ashford that they said were infant prodigies. I guess I'm as smart as they are, even if a lot younger, so am going to keep a diary myself.

The family can't read it, of course. They're awfully stupid. Heard mama say just now that the amah had better take me out, as I'm making marks all over a piece of paper on the dining-room floor. Will continue diary in kitchen. That's where I spend most of my time anyway.

I live in a nice brick house with my

family but though I have been introduced to the others, I am not well-acquainted with anybody except the amah. She speaks a nice, easy language and not the funny kind of foreign talk the others use. Am learning to understand them, though. This morning I heard them wondering where all last night's chicken went. But when I started to tell them about the cook's two cousins who are boarding in the kitchen, mama said, "Listen to the little dear. He's trying to say 'Daddy.'"

Have decided that the family is quite hopeless. Will learn to read the Want Ads as soon as possible so as to find a new home.

March 30

There are lots of things about grown-up talk that I don't understand yet. Today papa told my auntie that if she didn't make good pretty soon, he would send her back to America. Auntie cried and said that if papa would be decent to poor Bertie, she would soon have a man to care for her.

"Bertie!" said papa, "He isn't a man; he's a lap-dog." "He comes from a very good family!" Auntie said, crying some more.

"He must have come a long way," papa said.

"And he knows some of the best people in town," auntie replied.

"Perhaps. I always said myself that the night watchman was a pretty good fellow," papa remarked.

It's too deep for me. Am going to take a nap.

March 31

Went out today with the amah. Mama thought we went to the Public Gardens, but we didn't. Amah took me calling on Sinza Road where all her family live in a nifty two roomed house. They were very much interested in my new back tooth. First amah put her finger in my mouth. Then her brother, Lo Shing, First Rate Lady Best Style Tailor, put his finger in my mouth. Then her cousin, Ah See, who runs High Class Christian Gambling Parlor, put his finger in my mouth. Then Liou Zung, Stylish Maker of Ancient Chinese Ornament, put his finger in my mouth. Wish amah's family wasn't so fond of garlic.

April second

Went out with amah again this morning and a fresh Jap baby made a face at me in Hongkew Park. Will get even someday. When I was enjoying bottle at home later, mama said, "He's getting to be such a big baby that pretty soon we can give him solid food." If she only knew what I had this morning - piece of meat dumpling that amah chewed for me and a water chestnut. Amah is a good sport.

April third

Had colic. Squalled.

April fourth

Didn't sleep well last night, as father came home late and made lots of noise. Mama hasn't had much to say this morning. Very unusual. Looks like rain.

April fifth

Not much doing today. Papa asked mama

how her bridge party went. Mama said she lost five dollars. Papa said." Five dollars! Do you think I'm made of money?"

"Who dropped $200 on Silver Streak last fall?" Mama inquired sweetly. Papa turned red and murmured that accidents would happen. Mama said yes, they would, but that was no reason for betting on one of them. Papa picked up a poetry book, from the table in a hurry and started to read out loud. He read. "The stag at eve had drunk his fill."

"Yes," said mama, looking at Papa, "That is the worst of those stag parties."

Papa said he guessed he would go out and take a walk.

April sixth

Bertie called again today and said that he was not feeling well because a few months ago he had had a bad attack of water on the brain. Papa said it was too bad they removed it, as water is better than nothing. Auntie is not speaking to papa now. Grown-ups are very curious.

April sixth

Saw that fresh Jap baby again in Hongkew Park. Made a face at it. Mama said today that we might go to America soon, but that we can't take amah. Very sorry. Hate traveling with strangers. Believe I'll give the family my resignation and try to get a job.

April seventh

Raining again. Spent most of this morning in the basement with amah, watching houseboy and coolie play cards with mama's new bridge deck. Coolie won two pairs of papa's silk socks from houseboy. No use telling the family, though. They never listen to me.

April seventh

Afternoon and still raining. Papa was late to tiffin and mama said that he shouldn't have stopped in at the club. Papa said, "How did you know I stopped in at the club? By telepathy?"

"No," said mama, "I didn't have to use telepathy."

The girl next door passed just then with a man in an automobile, and papa said, "She seems to be getting by all right. Wonder why Ethel can't make it?"

"She's an impertinent little chit," said mama, looking out the window.

"Then I suppose you would call that fellow who fetches and carries for her a chit coolie," papa answered.

Nobody said anything more during tiffin. Slept in the afternoon and dreamt I hit that fresh Jap baby from Hongkew Park with my wooden elephant.

April eighth

Mama was real excited this morning, because she said that the stepsister to amah's grand-aunt had died and amah had to show up at the funeral.

"Who will take care of our baby?" mama asked.

"Oh, is that our baby?" said papa, looking surprised, "I always thought it was the amah's."

"Don't get funny," said mama, "It's a

serious proposition. She'll be gone all day. Somebody will have to look after him."

"There's a nomination I could make," papa said.

"You're trying to be ridiculous again. What would my friends think if they saw me wheeling a perambulator?"

"They might think you had a baby," papa said.

Mama didn't answer this right away, but remarked later that she wondered if amah really was going to a funeral.

"Maybe she belongs to the literary Section of the Amahs' Friday Morning Club and is going to read a paper on 'Introducing Chinese Civilization into the Foreign Home,'" papa remarked.

"You make me tired," said mama leaving the room.

Still sitting on the dining-room floor. Guess I'll have to shift for myself today.

April eighth

Didn't go out with mama after all. Rather sorry, as I believe in being democratic and cultivating the people I live with, even if I don't know them very well. Mama turned me over to the house-boy's aunt. Nice old party. Took me to a place where she burned some punksticks before a funny-looking gentleman; then undressed me and put some red paper on my chest for good joss. Didn't squall. Thought I'd humor the old girl.

Passed a place in Hongkew on way home, with pictures outside of black-haired man choking lady on top of building. Had glimpse of amah coming out with two other amahs, eating peanuts and giggling. Will snub her next time we meet.

April ninth

Nice weather again. Papa came downstairs after tiffin all dressed up in funny clothes and carrying a lot of clubs. "I'm going out to tee off," he said.

"That's all right, as long as you don't tee up," Mama answered.

Can't understand a lot of this talk. Wish they would try to learn my language.

April ninth (later)

Papa came in bye and bye. Said he saw Bertie on the links. "Yes, he is going to take Ethel and me to a dance tonight," said mama, "He goes to all the dances at the best cafes."

"And I suppose he takes part in all the most fashionable walks on the Bund and rides on the most exclusive streetcars," papa said.

Mama didn't say any more because funny noises came from downstairs just then, and papa said he was going down to the basement to tell that Chinese Mischa Elman to put some rosin on his bow.

April ninth (still later)

Nothing much else happened today, except that when I was going to bed I heard papa tell mama that he missed a lot of silk socks. "Is the houseboy wearing them to the meetings of the Young China Fantan Association or have ladies taken up half hose again?" he asked.

"You're always losing things," said mama, "What became of all that money you took out the other night to play poker with?"

"That's neither here nor there," papa said.

"It certainly isn't here," mama answered.

April ninth (last bulletin)

Have decided to forgive amah after all. Wish I could get a day off myself some times. Would like to start something with that fresh Jap baby that makes faces at me in Hongkew Park.

UNEXPURGATED DIARY OF A SHANGHAI BABY

Chapter II

In which the Baby Observes Family Life on Sunday Afternoon . . . He Observes That He Takes After Both Relations . . . The Mandarin Coat as a souvenir . . . First Battle in the Nippon-Baby War . . . The Mystery of the Shattered China.

April tenth

Sunday again. Like Sunday because there are so many papers on the floor for me to rattle, though family won't let me stay in living room very long. Tailor came this morning with new dress, and mama told papa that the Chinese have a genius for higher mathematics because they can take seven yards of georgette crepe, make a five-yard dress and have nothing left over. Papa said, "Uh-huh," and turned over the page of his pink sheet to see what Jiggs was doing.

"Look at baby with the newspaper," said Auntie, "Pretty soon he will be reading the comics."

"Yes," said mama, "If he can ever get them

away from his dad." Papa is still reading pictures. Guess I'll play with the Want Ad. section.

April tenth

Still Sunday. Auntie put record on phonograph and began to practice new dance. "I'll have to learn all the latest side-steps," said Auntie, "Dancing is getting more complicated than ever. Every little movement seems to have a meaning of its own."

"Yes," said papa, "And if some of the meanings were translated into words, they couldn't be sent through the mails. I've certainly seen some weird dancing in this town."

"Have you?" said mama looking interested, "I suppose you'll see some more of it when Ethel and I and the baby go away for the summer."

"Well," said papa, "the houseboy is a good fellow and he and I have many things in common, including my tobacco and silk socks, but that doesn't mean that I'm coming home early every evening you're away to play tiddledewinks with him."

Mama went out and banged door. Through with papers. Wish amah would come upstairs and bring me my wooden elephant. Want bite on back tooth.

April tenth

Sat on dining room floor during tiffin, as amah was busy in basement telling next-door amah all about Auntie's dates, Bertie, and mama's new dress. Papa said that if the houseboy didn't learn that he wanted to eat the food and not merely look at it, he was going to chain down the plates. He doesn't let a course pause in front of me any longer than the deacon halts the hat when taking up a collection at church," said papa.

"Maybe he is fussed because you are here," said mama, "He is not very fond of strangers."

"Well, if that cook was as good a performer on the kitchen range as he is on the Chinese piccolo, I wouldn't eat so many meals away from home," papa said.

I started to tell them a little later that I

wanted amah to come upstairs and give me some Chow.

"Listen to baby," mama said, "Isn't it funny how he talks all the time without saying anything?"

"I always said he took after you," said papa, reaching for hat and diving toward door.

"I'm not the only member of the family he takes after," mama shouted down the hall, "Have you ever noticed how fond he is of his bottle?"

Papa shut front door hard and went down street.

April tenth

Sunday afternoon. New man called to take Auntie to a place they called the Golden State.

"Who is that infant I saw Ethel going out with?" said papa, coming in just after they left. "Has she taken to teaching a kindergarten class?"

"He is no infant," said mama, "He was in the war two years and was wounded twice."

"I didn't know they mobilised the Boy Scouts," said papa, picking up the paper again.

Didn't hear any more because amah carried me off to take a nap.

April eleventh

Still raining some. Sat in basement while next-door amah told our amah all about the girl in her house. Didn't pay much attention, as was busy watching coolie wash his clothes with mamas perfumed complexion soap. Other amah went home bye and bye and our amah cracked some watermelon seeds for me. Pleasant morning.

April eleventh

Mama told papa at tiffin that she had gotten a letter from Aunt Lucy at home, asking her to send two or three Mandarin coats as souvenirs of China.

"Did she send a check with her little request?" papa asked. "Not so you could notice it," mama answered, shaking letter.

"They never do," said papa, "People at

home seem to think that all you have to do in China to get a Mandarin coat is to bait a trap with some chop suey and wait for a Mandarin to walk into it. Are you going to send her any?"

"No," said mama, "I've decided to wait until she goes to France this summer and then ask her to send me two or three little frocks from the Rue de la Paix as souvenirs of Paris."

"That's the stuff," said papa.

April eleventh (later)

Wish the rain would stop. Want to go out to Hongkew Park and settle things with that fresh Jap baby.

April twelfth

Feeling fine today. Amah parked my perambulator next to fresh Jap baby's in Hongkew Park, then went off to talk to Chinese policeman. Jap baby made face at me and tried to grab wooden elephant. First threw wooden elephant on ground out of reach, then leaned over and took Jap baby's bean-cake. Later reached for black hair and got some. Amah came back, picked up elephant, and wheeled me away. Who said Jap babies never bawl?

April twelfth (later)

Family more stupid than ever. Amah set me in bathroom this morning while she went for clean clothes, as I had spilled Jap bean-cake on dress. Saw upstairs coolie cleaning corners of wash-stand with mama's toothbrush. Squalled to call family. Mama came upstairs and asked amah if safety-pin was sticking me. No hope of getting across any real ideas in this house. Had pleasant nap later still holding black hair.

April thirteenth

Fair and warmer. Sat on porch today and watched new gardener pull up flowers and leave weeds. Papa said that Summer was coming and that he was going to hide his palm beach trousers before the amah kidnapped them to wear as part her summer sports costume. Nothing else happening except another new tooth in northwest corner of mouth. Wish I could try it out on Jap baby.

April fourteenth

Weather still good. Mama told papa at tiffin that amah said next door man on right was going to the States.

"Zat so?" said papa, telling boy to bring soup chop-chop. "His sole will be missed by every brass rail in Shanghai. There'll be lots of moaning at the bar when he puts out to sea."

Mama said that his friends held a farewell party at his house last night and that all the chinaware had been broken.

"Judging from his complexion this morning, they drank his farewell toast in Ningpo varnish," said papa.

"He'll have to behave for a while anyway, as he's going on an American liner and the only wet thing around the boat will be the ocean," mama replied. "He certainly is a wild character. It served him right to have all his chinaware broken."

Tried to tell family that next door houseboy had borrowed our China for party, but mama told amah to take me out as I was making too much noise.

April fifteenth

Mama found out about China today. Very angry. Papa said that if mama would look into the kitchen once in awhile, these things wouldn't happen. Mama said she stayed out of the kitchen as much as possible, because every time she went in, she found out something she didn't want to know. "Last time I dropped in, I saw the cook filling the chow water bottles from the kitchen faucet," mama said.

Houseboy says that he will make up loss by borrowing china from houses where his relations work. Mama remarked that she would, like to sack houseboy, but papa said never mind, as he is going to be married next week and will be punished enough.

April fifteenth (later)

Tried out new tooth on hard cake amah

bought from street hawker. Seems to be working well. Nobody else has noticed it, though. Wanted to call auntie's attention to it, but she was too busy talking to papa. Auntie was saying that she would like to invite Bertie to dinner.

"He doesn't have much chance to see home-life," Auntie said, "He lives in a mess."

"I don't doubt it," said papa, "He generally looks like one." Auntie said papa didn't appreciate Bertie, as he was very clever and was a great student of botany.

"I noticed that he was interested in grass widows," papa said.

"You don't know what a big soul he has, or you wouldn't say such things," said Auntie, beginning to cry.

"Don't I though," said papa, "I'll bet he wears number elevens."

Can't make anybody pay attention to tooth. Have thought some of squalling, but what is the use? They would only undress me to look for safety-pins.

Chapter III

In Which the Baby Finds that He Can't Stand the Social Pace . . . The Inconveniences of Being Kissed by Company . . . The Elusive Bachelor in Shanghai . . . Cold Jelly-Fish versus Stocking Feet.

APRIL sixteenth

Sleepy today, as family kept me awake last night getting ready to go to dinner party. Wish crib was up in attic. Noise began as soon as they came upstairs.

"Is it a boiled shirt affair?" asked papa, looking out of bathroom with lather on face.

"Of course," said mama, "Were you contemplating wearing your golf-suit?"

"I was contemplating not going at all," said papa, "Last time I went there a fat woman we played bridge with mistook my foot for her husband's and stepped on it every time they bid. I was lame for a week."

"You don't want to go any less than I do," said mama, "I went to a tea-party today and

UNEXPURGATED DIARY OF A SHANGHAI BABY

I'm all worn out."

"Well" said papa, looking at mama's evening dress, "If that's the way I felt about it, I'd put some clothes on and go to bed."

"Go on and get ready," said mama, jabbing tortoise shell ornament into hair. A few minutes later papa came back to ask if Ethel wasn't going.

"She's late again," said mama.

"I suppose she stopped to have a permanent wave put in her finger-nails or something," said papa, looking for pearl stud under bed. Just as they left I heard mama tell papa to keep an eye on the spoons, as she was trying to locate half a dozen that the house-boy loaned out a month ago. Have decided to start reprisals if family continues to make noise going to parties. Would like to organise other Shanghai babies into a union for an eight-hour day.

April 17th

Family came down late to break-fast on account of party. Mama told papa he should have known enough to return his partner's lead on hearts in the last rubber.

"I didn't realise I'd borrowed it from her," said papa. "It's too late to return it now unless I do it by chit. Besides, that will even us up a little. Her husband took $100 from me two months ago and hasn't returned it yet."

Mama didn't say anything but stirred coffee hard.

"Anyway," said papa after a moment, "I don't go through a whole hand with my mind in a millinery shop and then come up for air to ask what's trumps."

"Who does that?" asked mama sweetly.

"I read somewhere that the late Empress-Dowager did," said papa, looking at toast with interest. No more conversation during breakfast.

April 17th (later)

Company came in afternoon. Expected trouble when I heard mama tell amah to put on my filet lace dress, as I was to be brought downstairs for a while. Tried to crawl behind linen in closet, but amah found me and hauled me out. Hate company.

First fat woman kissed me and said I was a "diddle, diddle dumpkin." Then thin woman kissed me and said I was a "witchykitchy sweetheart." Then a bald-headed man kissed me and said I was a regular little Jack Dempsey.

"He's such a fine baby it's easy to see he has a mother's personal care," said one lady.

"He surely has," said mama looking pleased. Wonder if amah is a mother.

April 17th (still later)

Company finally drifted into next room to have tea and forgot me. Had a pleasant time playing with coal in brass hod and listening to conversation. Heard bald-headed man remark that he had a headache this afternoon, as he had taken several grains of quinine and it always made him dizzy. Surprised to hear this, as it was not quinine I noticed when he kissed me. He also said that he always takes a great deal of medicine in the East, as the drinking water doesn't agree with him.

"How did you happen to find out?" asked

papa politely. Mama kicked papa under table and started sudden conversation about expedition into Thibet.

"It must be terribly thrilling to be among wild people and wild animals," said fat lady.

"Oh, I don't know," answered papa, "You can see enough wild people here in Shanghai, and if you're pining for wild animals, just wait until the mosquito season opens."

"I think it must be very exciting," said mama, giving papa quick expression. "Sometimes I wish I had married an explorer."

"You have," said papa, reaching for cookie, "I'm just about to apply for a medal from the Royal Geographical Society. Yesterday, alone and unassisted, I found three addresses on Dixwell Road."

Thin lady said she heard that in Thibet they made statues of butter and kept them for as long as a year.

"Now I know where some of the dairies in Shanghai get their supply," said papa.

Went to sleep leaning against coal hod.

When I woke up, company had left to go to concert and mama was telling papa that he was hopelessly lowbrow.

April 18th

Bertie expected for dinner today. Auntie very excited. Bought some long-stemmed flowers and put them in vases on either side of the grate. Also spent hour before glass trying hair new way. I was downstairs when Bertie came and heard him remark that he was looking forward to going on a paper-hunt. "It's about time," said papa, who had come in from office. "I go on one six days a week, trying to pick up paper with some government printing on it. It's a great sport." Bertie said that he was thinking of giving up his present place to become a broker.

"Would you ride around town in one of those dear little traps?" asked Auntie, clasping her hands, "I think they're too sweet for words."

"Yes," said papa. "They're a great sight. Every morning the brokers stage a Ben Hur chariot race on the Bund, most of them standing up in the pose of an ancient Roman with short petticoats and a filet around his brow. Every time exchange drops a ha'penny, the mafoo hits the horse, and when it drops a penny, he runs over a ricsha coolie."

Didn't hear any more, as was busy pulling heads off long-stemmed flowers which flower-man had fastened on with pins.

April 19th

Fair weather this morning. Took off one more layer of clothes. Mama asked Auntie if Bertie had said anything yet. "Nothing except that it was a nice day yesterday," said Auntie, looking cross.

Auntie spent rest of morning playing sad music on phonograph. Papa came in for tiffin while she was trying "Where is My Wandering Boy Tonight?" and stood up straight with hand at forehead.

"Why are you standing up?" said mama, coming in.

"That's Shanghai's national anthem," said papa, sitting down at end of record.

Spent some time in basement with amah, trying to make friends with cook's cat. Rather nice pussy, but don't like the way he sings. Sounds like Auntie taking vocal culture.

April nineteenth

Heard mama tell papa that houseboy was going to be married in a few days and that family should give him a present.

"What's the idea?" asked papa.

"We don't owe him any present. He's been harvesting his trousseau from my wardrobe for the past three months."

Mama said if we lost this house boy, we might get another not interested in wardrobe but fond of family jewelry. Papa said that we might as well give him a present, as he would take one anyway.

"What shall it be - a silver nut dish or a brass card-receiver?" papa asked.

"Neither, of course," said mama.

"It ought to be something practical, that he could use every day."

"How about an alarm-clock?" asked papa.

Family still arguing when amah brought

my bottle and piece of candied ginger cousin sent from Canton.

April nineteenth

Quiet afternoon. Heard mama wondering why living-room couch always looked so untidy in the morning. Could have told her that cook's brother-in-law, who is out of job, sleeps there every night after family goes upstairs, but mama never talks to me unless to say "da-da" once in a while. Family rather snobbish. Glad amah and I move in same social circle.

April nineteenth

Papa came home early and mama told him that they were going to sukiaki with people they had met at card-party.

"Whose bright idea was that?" asked papa.

"Why, don't you like a sukiaki?" said mama.

"I can think of other ways of enjoying myself besides sitting in my stocking-feet on the floor eating Japanese stew and cold devilfish," said papa. "Besides, I never went to one of those affairs yet that I didn't have a hole in my sock, and had to walk with my feet drawn up, so people couldn't see it."

"That's your own fault," said mama.

"Oh, is it?" asked papa. "Well, if I'm expected to do the embroidery on my own hosiery, I may as well borrow some Chinese clothes and hire out as a Number 2 Amah."

Nothing more said about stockings just then, but later heard papa ask mama to lend him some court plaster as he had discovered hole.

April twentieth

Went out this morning with amah and wooden elephant. Elephant very nice to bite tooth on, but always falling out of perambulator into street. Amah kind about picking it up and giving it back to me. Know taste of every street in Shanghai.

CHAPTER IV

In Which the Baby Hears a Conversation on Art as She is Daubed . . . Later Observes the Chinese Art of Squeeze . . . Indications of Gentle Spring in the Far East . . . Why Caesar crossed the Rubicon.

April twentieth

Mama received picture from America, which she said Aunt Mary sent her for anniversary present. "Isn't it a wonderful work of art?" said mama, showing it to papa.

"It surely is," said papa, turning frame, "Which way do you look at it?"

"It's a view of the sun setting behind waves," said mama, snatching it away.

"Oh, is it?" asked papa. "I thought it was a ripe tomato rising above a sheaf of lettuce leaves."

Mama said papa had no appreciation of art, and papa said that he had and could prove it by bringing home picture which friend had just given him called "Nymph

Among the Flowers."

"I'm not sure we would want that in our home," mama answered.

"Oh, it's perfectly O.K.," papa said. "It was done after the Futurist School and might just as well have been entitled, 'Electrical Buzz Saw in Action.'"

Family stopped talking about pictures, as washman come just then and mama wanted to know why all family linen had changed initials in last five days.

April twenty-first

Pleasant weather. Sat on porch with wooden elephant and watched our coolie cut flowers from next-door garden. Later coolie came in and collected twenty cents from mama to pay flower-man. Just wait until I can talk.

April twenty-first

Auntie said at tiffin today that she was going to tea-dance with new man named Cyril.

"Everybody says that he is a wonderful

dancer," said Auntie, "He has made a name for himself."

"He has made several names for himself, and he uses them when he signs chits," said papa.

"I think you are too mean for words," said Auntie, struggling to cut chop.

"Well," said papa, "I wouldn't pin too much faith to a wonderful dancer. You can't eat a foxtrot."

Mama said it was a good thing young men in town had the habit of hiring cars, as a girl couldn't make much progress otherwise on account of ricshas being so unsociable.

"They ought to build them tandem," said papa.

When family stopped talking about ricshas, papa remarked that mama ought to tell the cook not to buy any more Peking camels, as he had blisters on his hands from trying to cut the meat.

April twenty-first

Nice afternoon. Went out with amah in perambulator. Saw fresh Jap baby on Jap amah's back. Looked very foolish. Glad I don't have to wear kimono in street.

April twenty-first

Came home later and saw Cyril arrive to take Auntie to tea dance. Neighbor lady also calling.

"Isn't Shanghai just too cosmopolitan for anything?" said Auntie, sitting on edge of chair and starting conversation.

Didn't hear more, as mama remarked to neighbor lady that amah had kept me out a long time that afternoon, but that she didn't mind because the fresh air did me good. Amah didn't say that we spent afternoon with other amahs in moving-picture show, seeing fine film of lady tied to railroad track by gentleman.

April twenty-second

Nice day. Mama took accounts with cook this morning, and when papa came home at noon she showed him grocery bill.

"Do you think we could have eaten as much as that?" she said.

UNEXPURGATED DIARY OF A SHANGHAI BABY

"Not unless we kept an orphan asylum," said papa, reading total. "He must have added in the average annual rainfall and the gross tonnage of the Empress of Asia."

"We'd better not be too hard on him," said mama. "Maybe we do eat more than we realize. Only this morning he showed me that the coffee can was empty again."

Guess cook didn't mention dipping out of can every day to fill two other cans on shelf. Probably amah will keep me out of kitchen when family begins to understand my language.

April twenty-third

Raining. Mama and papa talked at breakfast about dinner they will give next week for taipan. Mama said that they will have to invite one more man and suggested friend in mess.

"I've heard people say that he's pretty good in a party," said mama.

"He is in some ways but I've noticed that when the chits come around, he always gets writers' cramp," said papa.

Mama said that they would have to ask him, as there wasn't much time left, and that she would send coolie over with note.

"If you're in a hurry, you'd better mail it," said papa, starting for office.

Mama went out herself soon afterwards, because she told Auntie that she was going to try to find a spring hat under fifty dollars that didn't look as if it had gone through the Kansu earthquake.

April twenty-third (afternoon)

Still raining in afternoon. Lady who writes poetry called after tiffin and asked papa if he had observed the evidences of spring.

"Yes," said papa, "I've noticed that all the drugstores have taken in the cold remedies and are featuring the cholera cures."

"Haven't you observed other indications?" asked lady, looking disappointed.

"The ricsha coolies are taking off more clothes," said papa.

"But surely you feel a thrill of happiness because winter is over," lady said. "Doesn't it mean something to you?"

'It means something to me, but it doesn't give me a thrill of happiness," papa answered, "It means that pretty soon I'll have to wear a monkey-jacket, and every time I put one on, I feel that I ought to pick up the card-tray and page somebody."

Mama came downstairs just then, and papa sneaked out toward Race Course. Wish he'd take me some time. Tired of going to park and hearing amahs talk about new family that just moved to Frenchtown.

April twenty-fourth

Sunday, sat on floor in living room and heard family talk about next-door automobile.

"I wish we had a car," said mama, looking out window.

"Why?" asked papa. "We don't know anybody in Woosung."

"There are plenty of places to go besides Woosung," said mama.

"No place that I know except the Rubicon," said papa, "and I've been around that so many times that I don't wonder Julius Caesar got impatient and crossed it instead."

"It isn't so much a question of where you can go as the impression a motor car makes on members of the community," mama answered.

Papa said yes, that most cars did make impressions on members of the community, but they were usually made on Chinese members that didn't jump fast enough.

Mama picked up fashion-paper and turned leaves with rattle.

April twenty-fourth, later

Had pleasant nap upstairs, but woke up later and saw coolie trying on mama's new spring hat before mirror. I'd just like to catch him putting on my bonnet!

Chapter V

In Which the Baby Finds That a Dinner Party Takes as Much Preparation as a Battle and is About the Same Thing in the End . . . The Diplomatic House-Boy Gets a Line on the Taipan's Dinner Clothes . . . Papa's Friend Believes in Preparedness.

April twenty-fifth

Went out calling on amah's third cousin who lives on little street near Nanking Road. Perfumes very unusual. Not a bit like mama's talcum. Don't remember much of visit, as went to sleep on bed with Chinese baby getting over mumps. Later amah let me drink tea from her cup and gave me piece of fried dumpling. Pleasant morning.

April twenty-sixth

Nobody paying any attention to me today. Everybody getting ready for taipan's dinner. Amah busy making red paper frills. Mama busy making place cards. Cook busy making menu. Auntie busy making complexion. Houseboy busy making trouble. Hope they don't forget my chow.

April twenty-sixth, later

Papa came home to tiffin and brought fresh lettuce.

"It's perfectly safe," he said "One of the men in the office grew it in his own garden."

"I'm so glad," said mama. "I'm as hungry for lettuce as a rabbit. I'll send it right down to the cook to get ready for tonight."

Sat in kitchen later while amah tried on Paris garters she had found in papa's bureau drawer. Had interesting time watching cook blow mouthfuls of water on sanitary lettuce to keep it fresh.

April twenty-sixth

Still sitting in living-room. Family forgot to have me put to bed. Table all ready for taipan's party. Mama called downstairs to papa and asked him what he was doing.

"Reading a love-story in the Municipal

Gazette." said papa. "Can't I sit down for five minutes without giving an account of myself?"

"Go in the dining-room and compare the place-cards with the initials on the knives and forks," said Mama. "The houseboy borrowed from all over so as not to have dish-washing between courses and I want to make sure that nobody gets his own silver."

Mama said later that she had decided upon everything except the person who was to sit on papa's left.

"Well, don't go and pick out a century plant," said papa, taking salted peanut from red paper dish. "The last one you put me next to remembered the inauguration of Lincoln."

Squalled at this point and was taken upstairs, but couldn't sleep anyway on account of noise. Heard papa ask mama what had become of his pearl studs.

"I gave them to the baby for cough-drops," said mama, with unpleasant look in voice.

Papa said all right, that she didn't need to

tell him if she didn't want to, but if he didn't find them he would wear my safety pins.

April twenty-sixth, last bulletin

Papa wondering if taipan would wear evening suit or dinner coat.

"If he wears a dress suit, I don't want to show up in a dinner coat, and if he comes in a dinner coat, I don't want to put something over on him by wearing an evening suit," said papa.

Mama said he might send the houseboy over to ask taipan's houseboy what his master was putting on.

"I'm afraid he'd tip it off to the taipan," said papa.

Mama said she didn't think so, and that anyway the Orientals have a grand reputation for diplomacy. Houseboy went, but came back pretty soon. Told papa that other master sent compliments and said he would wear evening dress and that his wife was going to wear low-necked purple gown with pearl necklace. Did not catch papa's remark, but heard shoe falling downstairs after houseboy. Sometime when feeling good, I will get even with family by squalling all night.

April twenty-seventh

Everybody cross today after taipan's dinner. Papa said party would have been a success if houseboy had not served dinner from behind heavy garlic barrage. Mama said it was papa's fault for telling story he had heard at club and for spearing olives with fork. Auntie cross because Bertie led her aside to say something special and then asked her for piece of baby-ribbon to tie up his lampshade.

Cook cross because people ate so much that he had nothing left over for cousins. Family living today on salted peanuts, fudge, and ripe olives. Glad we don't have dinners often.

April twenty-eighth

Had interesting morning sitting on living-room floor and trying new tooth on carved wood screen. Heard mama remark that she had met papa's friend and that he looked as if he were going to be best man at a hanging.

"He is upset because he is going home on the Golden State," said papa.

He is afraid his suitcases will leak. "Is the Golden State going to be dry?" asked mama.

"Theoretically, yes," said papa, "but thus far there have been 103 more tons of baggage than freight shipped on board, and practically all of it would splash if roughly handled."

"But won't they be caught by the Department of Justice when they land in San Francisco?" asked mama.

"Oh, no," said papa. "By the time they reach San Francisco, it will be a case for the Department of the Interior."

Spent part of afternoon sitting in pen on porch and hearing mama tell the neighbor lady that her hair had come out something terrible since living in Shanghai and that pretty soon she would not have enough for sidepuffs.

April twenty-eighth

Papa came home later feeling very happy, and said that he had seen friend off on Golden State.

"He must have unpacked his suit-cases rather soon," mama remarked.

"Oh no," said papa, looking at self in glass. "All the Elijahs who tried to protect themselves against the drought will have a lot more than a little oil. They put a bar on at Hongkong."

Mama said that she was glad there was a place where papa's friend could settle down with his knitting and feel at home.

Chapter VI

In Which the Baby, Hears about the Carlton and Proposals . . . Papa Tries Going in a Pool . . . Auntie has Idea for Safe and Sane Bet . . . Bridge as a Means of Promoting Harmony.

April twenty-ninth

Not much doing today. Spent part of morning in basement, hearing coolie play music on Chinese fiddle. Very good noise. Couldn't do better myself.

April twenty-ninth

Auntie upset today because she heard Bertie was going with girl in Frenchtown. Papa asked if Auntie had ever seen her.

"Yes, she was at the Carlton the other night," said Auntie. "She was the one who didn't have enough clothes on and who danced so funny."

"You don't expect me to pick her out from that, do you?" asked papa. "The description fits ninety percent of the women there."

Auntie said she thought girl's dress was old-fashioned.

"Most of them were dressed from the waist up in the most old-fashioned clothes there are," said papa.

Auntie said she thought papa was impolite and remarked that anyway she didn't care about Bertie, as there were plenty of other men. "A man proposed to me on the boat coming over," said Auntie.

"What was the matter with him?" asked papa, "Was he seasick?"

"He was nothing of the sort," said Auntie, with mad edge in voice. "He asked me to marry him the third day out."

"I'll bet he didn't say it loud enough for you to hear him," said papa, eating 205th salted peanut.

Auntie said that anyway she knew Cyril was in love with her, as she could tell by the way he looked at her when she wasn't looking at him. Papa told her that her periscope seemed to be in pretty good working order, but that she ought to be careful not to get a kink in her neck.

April thirtieth

Pleasant day. Amah, cook, houseboy, and coolie excited about something called sweep-stake. Nobody paid much attention to me, but not sorry as had found can of syrup that oozed at top.

"I'm going in a Pool with the fellows at the office," said papa, coming in for tiffin.

"Isn't it rather early for swimming?" asked mama, looking up from Ladies Home Journal.

Papa started to say something, but stopped and remarked that yes, it was, but this time he was hoping to pick up a little seaweed.

Wish he'd give some to me, as would like to see if it is good to try on new tooth.

May first

Not much doing today. Sat in dining-room for awhile trying to lick color off of red and blue round things which I found on floor. Color didn't come off very well. Later stayed in kitchen with amah while cook was fixing tiffin. Cook's cat took piece of fish from shelf and began to eat it on floor. Cook took fish away from cat and put it on frying pan. Was surprised cat was hungry, as had heard papa tell friend that he had sat up most of the night feeding the kitty.

May first

Mama cross at tiffin. Told papa that the lowbrow friends he met at the club had no place in a proper home.

"That tall one who just came out from the States is round-shouldered from getting in and out of patrol-wagons," said mama.

Papa said that some of mama's friends were not so many laps ahead and that stout lady was so uncultured that she thought "The Lays of Ancient Rome" had something to do with eggs.

"Besides, she's so fat that she has to ride around in two ricshas," papa remarked.

No more noise during tiffin.

May second

Rain. Stayed home and heard coolie play fiddle. Mama said that the only thing worse than man learning to play cornet was man learning to play Chinese musical instrument.

"The trouble is you never can tell when they've learned," said papa.

Hope coolie doesn't get into habit, as family couldn't tell difference in case I wanted to squall for something.

May second

Papa didn't go to office this afternoon on account of races. Asked Auntie if she wanted to put up a bet. "Will they give me my money back in case my horse doesn't win?" Auntie inquired.

"Of course," said papa. "Do you think they would be mean enough to keep it?"

Auntie said that she had read a lot about race-course sharks and wanted to be careful.

May second

Still raining. Nothing to do but stay

home with wooden elephant and watch coolie sweep dust under living-room lounge. Papa came home later, and mama asked him if his favorite had won.

"That horse was so slow coming in that the judges thought he was winning the next race," said papa, pulling off gloves with unpleasant look. "He certainly was one poor runner."

"How much did it cost you to find that out?" asked mama, but papa had started upstairs to get money out of mama's purse for ricsha man.

May third

Sat in dining-room and heard family talk about bridge they had gone to at place called Columbia Country Club. Papa remarked that the family scores, taken together, about equalled the number of votes a cross-eyed girl would get in a beauty-contest.

"It's too bad we didn't play mah-jong instead," said mama. "We might have won the mah-jong set."

"Yes," papa answered. "Think of all the fun the baby could have had swallowing the counters."

Papa said after a moment that he always had been keen about bridge.

"I love the sprightly conversation that goes during a bridge game and the kindly looks that are exchanged among the players," papa remarked. "I am also fond of the lady who holds a coroner's inquest over every hand and digs back 13 tricks to call you to time for not having led the fourth best of your strongest suit. The only time I'm happy playing bridge is when I'm the dummy."

"That's because you feel so natural," said mama.

Papa started to say something, but began to whistle "Kiss Me Again" and went out to office.

May third

Family all worked up at tiffin because I said "Daddy," Nothing to get excited over, as have been saying it for past month. Only trouble is that family never listens to me.

May third, later

Auntie went out to races with Cyril. Came home afterwards and Papa asked her how she had liked them.

"Oh, they were fine," said Auntie. "I saw the cutest duvetyn dress cut Directoire, and a perfectly stunning lavender raincoat with a white rubber flower on the hat."

"But who won the races?" asked papa.

"Oh, a lot of horses," said Auntie, pulling out hatpin. "I don't know their names."

Papa said that if Auntie went to an execution, she probably wouldn't know if the man was being shot for stealing jade or for passing another automobile on Nanking Road.

Chapter VII

In Which the Baby is Perturbed by Cucumbers and the Spring Meet . . . The Pleasures of House-Booting . . . The Jap Baby Springs a New Accomplishment, Thereby Upsetting Some Deep-laid Plans.

May fourth

Everybody gone to races to-day. Cook took bird-cage and went after tiffin. Houseboy went to dentist for tooth-ache, but saw dentist at same place. Nobody home but amah and me. Pretty soon amah put me in perambulator and wheeled me to house of old Chinese lady, then went out toward Bubbling Well. Old lady gave me nice piece of cucumber to chew, which she told amah wouldn't hurt me because it was too big for me to swallow. Fooled her. Swallowed it. Would like to live in this house, as would enjoy chickens roosting on crib.

May fourth, later

Amah came back in hurry, wheeled me in rear entrance of home, took off bonnet, and had me sitting in pen when family came in front way. Told mama I had slept upstairs all afternoon. Surprised that amah has such poor memory.

Papa said that married men always lost, as he had won $50 in Pari-Mutuel, but had to spend $250 to dress up family for races.

"Anyway, a lot of people looked at me in my new clothes," said mama.

Papa said a lot more would have looked at her if she had just blacked her face, and it wouldn't have been nearly as expensive.

Cyril came in bye-and-bye, looking unhappy. Said that he had been tipped off on a pony.

"Did you hurt yourself much when you fell?" asked Auntie.

"About a hundred dollars' worth," said Cyril.

Auntie said it was awful the way the doctors charge in this town and that Cyril should be more careful in his riding.

May fifth

Something wrong inside. Squalled all day. Mama said climate doesn't agree with me. Don't remember eating any climate.

May sixth

Somewhat better. Went out with amah to Hongkew Park and saw fresh Jap baby. Looked in other direction as am not feeling in good trim yet.

May sixth

Family talking about invitation to go on houseboat trip. Mama asked papa if he would like to go.

"Why should I?" asked papa. "All I have to do is to take the springs out of my bed and saw off the end so that I have to sleep doubled up like a Duplex apartment. Then I need only tell the boy to break all the bottles of chow water and forget some important articles of diet; limit the family to one washbasin; hire some fragrances strong enough to walk up and shake hands; and engage a lot of coolies to look in the window while I'm dressing, and I can have just as much fun as if I were on a houseboat trip. I never went on a houseboat party yet where the boy didn't break the water-bottles. It must be a rule in the Chinese civil code."

Mama said that papa probably didn't miss the water-bottles very much, and papa said that he wouldn't get the credit for it even if he did. Papa remarked later that families who went on houseboat parties together either parted mortal enemies or else had so much on each other that they had to stay good friends.

May seventh

Nice day. Sat in kitchen and watched cook scrub potatoes with old hair-brush. Later enjoyed pleasant time while cook's wife and amah had argument over winnings on Pari-mutuel ticket. Cook's wife bit amah's ear. Many remarks about ancestors. Busy morning.

May seventh, later

Mama remarked at tiffin that hot weather

would soon be here and that papa ought to buy a pith helmet.

"I have no ambition to go around town looking like Livingston exploring Africa," said papa. "The chief thing I am going to get for the hot weather is a little printed card saying, 'No, I wouldn't mind the heat if it wasn't for the humidity'. By pinning it to my lapel I'll be saved the trouble of saying it 999 times a day."

"What will you find to talk about?" asked mama.

"Just watch me," said papa.

Mama remarked that she had every intention of doing so.

May seventh

Papa came home wearing court plaster on countenance. Said he was going to find new barber as he was tired of losing so much face.

Think court-plaster would be very becoming to Jap baby. Will practice throwing wooden elephant so as to be ready for next trip to Hongkew Park.

May eighth

Not much doing today. Had pleasant time upstairs while family went for ride in car, watching houseboy take shave with papa's new safety razor. Later saw him put on some of mama's Mary Garden perfume. Perfume had hard fight with garlic. Garlic won. Will try to keep an eye on my talcum powder.

May eighth

Family came home later and mama said she didn't see why we couldn't have car too, as she was tired paying coppers in tram and having them handed back because of wrong pictures.

'If you'd just say 'season,' you wouldn't have to pay any coppers," said papa. "Nobody who knows the ropes pays to ride in a tram in this city."

Mama said that if papa was the right sort, he would buy her a car. Papa answered that if he did it would have to be cheap one without a self-starter, and he had trouble enough already cranking up the telephone.

May eighth, later
Sat on floor with wooden elephant while family ate tiffin. Surprised to hear papa say that trains during war were protected by amah. Didn't know she traveled.

May ninth
Went out to Hongkew Park and saw fresh Jap baby wearing white apron on top of kimono and little flat red hat on head. Silly get-up. Jap family excited because baby could step alone. Awfully stuck on itself. Have decided not to throw wooden elephant, as didn't know Jap baby could walk.

May ninth
Papa came home for tiffin and mama told him about new sweater which Aunt at home had sent her.

"It would be nice to have Aunt Mary come out to visit us," said mama.

"I don't think she would like the Soochow bathtubs," said papa with unhappy look. "Nobody but a cobra could be comfortable in one."

"I had no intention of asking her to sleep in a Soochow bath-tub," said mama, giving papa quick expression, "If she was your aunt, you'd want to give her the best room, but just because she's mine you don't care what becomes of her."

Papa said that there are ants enough around in the summer-time eating up the provisions, without sending for another from America.

May ninth

Had busy time later chinning self on side of pen. Will walk soon if lucky. Afterwards went upstairs for nap and saw new coolie mopping floor with mama's mamma's sweater on broom-stick. Pleasant afternoon.

May tenth

Nice day. Mama has taught amah to put funny glass thing in my mouth and then read what it says. Told amah she must cook it first.

Amah cooks it, then tastes it to see if it is all right before giving it to me. Can't find any sense in stunt, but then have stopped expecting much of family.

May eleventh

Family had busy time today talking about place to go for summer. Papa said he would like to go somewhere where there is good hunting. Mama answered that he could find that in any resort and he wouldn't have to go out of his room, either.

Papa said later that he hoped to find place where shoes were something to put on feet and not ground for green vegetable garden.

"Why not ask our friends about good places?" asked mama.

"We might try it, but I've noticed that people are always strongest for the resorts they haven't visited," papa answered.

Rather looks at present as if family is going to Tsingtao. Hope so, as might find Jap babies there that haven't learned to walk. Have decided to save wooden elephant.

May twelfth

Papa said that tomorrow would be Friday

the thirteenth and Auntie asked him if he was superstitious.

"Yes," said papa, "I always used to hate to get thirteen days in jail for speeding and I never do like to pay bills that fall due on Friday."

Auntie said she didn't wish anybody any bad luck, but that she hoped girl from French-town would fall down at tea dance and sprain her costume.

Chapter VIII

In Which the Baby Decides That the Life of Infant in Shanghai is One Round of Friday, the Thirteenth . . . New Hope for the Jessfield Monkey-House . . . The Baby Tries to Help Out a Romantic Situation.

May twelfth

Porch covered with woolen things being aired for summer. Mama said she was going to put them in moth-proof bags. Papa said that amah-proof box would be more to point. Wish there was such a thing as amah-proof baby.

May thirteenth

Friday today. Family said day means bad luck. Can't see that luck is any worse than usual. Stuck by same number of safety-pins and have same funny feeling in mouth where new tooth is coming. Amah very busy telling all other amahs in town about family going to Tsingtao for summer. Papa told mama at tiffin that she must be raising me on cafeteria plan, as there wasn't anybody to wait on me. Didn't mind being left alone, as was busy upstairs watching new coolie clean bathtub with mama's crocheted washcloth.

May thirteenth

Mama asked papa if he had had any bad luck today.

"Every day is Friday the thirteenth to a married man," said papa, reading bill for mama's new dress. Mama said that she could have married half a dozen nice men at home, and papa said it was too bad she didn't as she needed that many to pay for clothes. Auntie said just then that papa didn't realise how expensive clothes were, as she had just paid ten dollars a yard for dress to wear to Carlton.

"That oughtn't to be too expensive," said papa. "You don't need more than a yard."

Mama answered that she was not going around town looking like wife of a poor man, and papa replied that poor men's wives were best-dressed women in Shanghai, as that was why husbands were poor.

May thirteenth

Had interesting ride in perambulator. Passed Hangkew Market and saw poultry man make dead ducks fat by blowing up at windpipe. Also saw fish-men painting fresh red gills on old-fashioned fish. Later had glimpse of family cook doing shopping. Glad I take my tiffins out of a bottle.

May thirteenth

Papa come home early and had busy time trying to get number on telephone. Mama told him he should be ashamed to swear in front of baby.

"Turn the baby around," said papa.

"These gentlemen hello-girls make all the connections by absent treatment," papa remarked, after saying prayers. "We're so used to not getting the number that if all the staff walked out on strike Shanghai people wouldn't know it until they read it in the paper. You stand about as much chance of getting the right number on a Shanghai telephone as you do in the Sweepstake."

Papa remarked later that people who

wandered forty years in wilderness were probably trying to get the land of Canaan on the telephone.

"There weren't any telephones in Bible times," said mama.

"Of course there were," said papa. "Didn't you ever hear of the Book of Numbers?"

Central interrupted then to tell papa that line was engaged and also out of order. Amah carried me out in hurry.

May fourteenth

Pleasant day. Sat on porch while amah pulled out her front hair with string and patted pieces of black court plaster on forehead for headache. Papa came home for tiffin and Auntie asked him if he was going in for any kind of spring athletics.

"No," said papa. "I get plenty of exercise sprinting into the house after paying a ricsha coolie, so as to arrive ahead of the row. I used to be a shark at baseball, but I haven't any time to practice."

"You are still good at catching high-balls," said mama. Papa said he was glad to hear mama admit that he was good at something. Rest of tiffin quiet except for soup.

Papa remarked later after finding coolie brushing bureau with silk shirt that he was sorry ratepayers wouldn't allow Municipal Council to build the $10,000 monkey-house in Jessfield Park, as he would like to contribute new upstairs coolie and might also be persuaded to part with house-boy.

May fourteenth

Had ride to Hongkew Park. No sign of Jap baby. Hope it is walking back to Japan.

May fifteenth

Nice day. Family excited because I said "Mama." Was really trying to say "Amah" but can't make family understand my language. Papa said that mama had better pay a little more attention to me when I begin to talk.

What about my bridge parties? asked mama.

"Teach the baby to score and then you can take him with you," said papa. "If he stays in the back of the house all the time, he will learn to swear in Chinese."

"Yes, and if he stays in the front of the house, he will learn to swear in English," said mama, looking at papa. Papa said that he guessed he had a right to say something when he found that houseboy had put flypaper in bureau drawer to keep moths away from golf-socks.

May fifteenth, later

Sat on floor while family read paper. Auntie asked meaning of "P.P.C." which she had seen in corner of friend's card.

"I've heard that it means 'Please Postpone Chits'," said mama.

"I've also known cases where it stood for 'Payment Permanently Cancelled'," papa remarked.

Mama said family would have to send steamer present to friends and suggested basket of flowers.

"Yes," said papa. "People in a state-room so small that they have to sleep with their hats on because they have no place to put them always appreciate a basket of flowers. Besides, it is such a comfort when you have 31½ pieces of hand luggage to have a kind friend rush up and make it 32½."

Mama remarked that she might send box of candy, only friend would not appreciate it after the first day out. "I'll look around the house and try to find something that I don't use very often and wouldn't miss much," mama said.

"Why not send them the baby?" papa inquired.

No more remarks about present. Papa said later that maybe friends would not appreciate family coming to see them off, as many people preferred to stay inside tender until it got too far away from jetty for shroffs to jump.

May sixteenth

Amah bought me new black rubber thing today. Thought I was getting chow, but found out it was bluff. Disappointed to find no connection. Wonder if they think they are really fooling me. Wouldn't hold it in Hongkew Park, as didn't want Jap baby to think I was being taken in.

May seventeenth

Pleasant weather. Auntie said this morning that Cyril had invited her to go to lecture on "Theory of Relativity."

"Do you know what that is?" she asked mama.

"I don't know for certain, but I think it is about how to get along with your relatives," mama said.

Hope they all go. Maybe they'll learn more about getting along with Me.

May eighteenth

Had pleasant trip to Hongkew Park. Rubber thing fell out of perambulator. Hoped I had lost it, but amah picked it up again.

Flavor of Hongkew Park not as good as Public Garden. Later came home and watched amah's younger sister hand starch mama's white kid gloves.

May eighteenth, later

Weather still good. Papa said he had to hurry at noon, as he and lawyer friend at club were going to look into important case that had just come up. Mama asked him if important case had just come up from cellar. Quiet tiffin.

May nineteenth

Bertie called this afternoon. Said he was sorry to have stayed away so long, but that he had sprained shoulder.

"Yes, I've heard she dances like that," said Auntie with ice-box expression.

Bertie pulled collar as face turned color of Jap baby's felt hat. Then asked Auntie why she went with Cyril person.

"There is nothing the matter with Cyril," said Auntie, tossing head. "He goes in the best society in Poo-tung."

Bertie asked Auntie what Cyril did for a living, and Auntie said she wasn't sure but thought he handled remittance department in some bank, as she had heard he was remittance man.

Bertie tried to hold Auntie with arm and Auntie said she would scream if he didn't stop. Tried to help by squalling to call family. Bertie pulled collar again and said he would have to go home. Went. Auntie said I was a pest and ought to be locked up in garret. Can't understand family. Guess I'll go to sleep with wooden elephant and make-believe chow.

Chapter IX

In Which the Baby is First Introduced to Mr. Henli Regatta . . . Mama Brings Happiness to the American Navy . . . The Baby Goes on Spree at Theater and Mah-Jongg Party . . . Peanuts as an Infant Diet.

MAY twentieth

Too many clothes for weather. Wish amah would dress me like Auntie. Had nap upstairs while coolie tried mama's cold cream on complexion. Amah caught him. Told him he should be ashamed to take mama's things and that anyway she had seen bottle first. Coolie came back later and took drink of mama's florida water. Seemed very happy. Much Chinese music. Wish they'd let me have nap, as being baby in Shanghai is not easy job.

May twentieth

Auntie excited at tiffin, as black cat had crossed path. Asked papa if he believed in signs.

"Not in Shanghai," said papa. "I waited for fifteen minutes for a tram this morning at a place called a 'Request Stop.' Next time I'll send my request in five days in advance and get the seal of the Minister of Communications in Peking."

Auntie said she didn't mean that kind of signs, but wanted to know if black cat had any connection with bad luck. Papa said it often did, as he had caught cook's cat drinking cream several times and it had always meant bad luck for the cat.

Mama said that upstairs coolie had broken shaving mirror that morning, as he seemed excited and was working in hurry to go away to Chinese funeral. Papa said that if he wasn't more careful he would soon go to another one, only nobody would expect him to light joss sticks. No more conversation about coolie, as papa stopped to tell houseboy that though he was fond of soup, he didn't like it on collar-bone.

May twentieth, later

Went out for jaunt in perambulator with amah. Amah very good chauffeur. Pushes ricsha coolies out of way with conversation. Saw Jap baby in front of bath-house and hoped He would get lots of soap in mouth. Later passed Auntie and girl friend, but was cut dead. Hate these social distinctions.

May twenty-first

Nice day. Auntie busy getting new clothes to wear Sunday when she goes to see somebody called Henli Regatta. Don't know Henli. Must be new friend.

Auntie said all ready-made clothes she had tried on fitted like an Underwood typewriter cover on a Corona.

Mama told her she should be careful not to speak of typewriters, as it wouldn't do to let Shanghai people know that she had had job in office of coal and feed store at home.

"I've been introducing you as somebody with money, and you ought to help out in the impression," mama said.

"Haven't I been trying to?" asked Auntie.

"I write all my letters on Astor House stationery and when I am at a tea, I always call up on the telephone to find out why my car hasn't come."

Mama remarked that when next door girl said she couldn't bear to be dictated to Auntie spilled beans by saying that she couldn't either, unless the boss spoke very slowly. Surprised to hear of Auntie spilling beans, as had never seen her in kitchen.

May twenty-first, later

Papa came home for afternoon. Mama told him that if family was going to Tsingtao, he would have to go down to American Consulate and get a passport.

"The trouble is that if I go to American Consulate, I'll also have to pay my income tax and I haven't seen anything coming in except shroffs," said papa.

Mama remarked that it would probably be pretty hard for papa to figure up his income, and papa said no, it wouldn't, as all he would have to do would be to add up what mama had spent.

No more conversation for a while, but afterwards papa said that he would have to stay in town during part of summer and play tag with mosquitoes.

"I hope you'll promise not to take more than one cocktail at a time while we're away," mama remarked.

Papa said that would be easy, as he always found it awkward to lift two glasses at once.

"It will be rather hard to take the baby up to Tsingtao," said mama.

"Why not put him in mothballs with the furs?" papa inquired. No answer from mama.

May twenty-first

Couldn't go to Hongkew this afternoon as park is busy holding sailors. Mama told papa that she was going to picnic and would bring enough food for five navy men.

"You'd better hire half a dozen ricshas," said papa. "The cargo capacity of the American navy is the highest in the world."

Mama said she was taking macaroons and heart- shaped sandwiches, also mint candies. Papa remarked that on that diet, the U. S. Navy would soon be in shape to win a push-ball contest from Montenegro. Mama said that she hoped she would be asked to help decide male beauty contest, as she was a competent judge of handsome men.

"Yes," said papa. "You surely gave me a life sentence at hard labor."

Mama told papa that he had wrong impression and had probably gotten it by shaving in front of Auntie's picture of Francis Bushman since coolie broke mirror.

May twenty second

Nobody home today. All gone to see Henli regatta. Family left in hurry this morning after Auntie changed dress four times and complexion twice. Auntie said she had put on medium tint, and papa said that described it, as it was certainly neither rare nor well done. Mama remarked that she lets her color come and go, and papa answered yes, that it comes on in the morning and goes off at night.

"It's too bad we didn't get an invitation to

go on a houseboat," said mama.

Papa said that the boats were very crowded and that they would have had as much privacy as an elephant in zoo, also that he would probably be expected to sleep on hatch. Auntie finally said she was going to wear a fluffy summer girl's costume, and papa remarked that it would probably be all right as long as the fluffy summer didn't catch her in it.

Family went out at last and banged door, after Auntie came back twice to put more powder on nose and once to put perfume behind ear. Heard papa say that it was a shame to waste two good bottles on pickles but mama told him to stop talking and call a car.

"The kind of car this family is going to travel in passes the corner every five minutes without being called," said papa.

Mama said that he was as tight with his money as Auntie's new shoes, but papa said that all he had left after buying railroad tickets was a dollar with copper filling and he was saying that for church.

May twenty-second

Pleasant day. Houseboy, cook, coolie, and relations having game on dining-room table with family's mah-jong set. Amah trying on papa's silk socks left by houseboy. Amah's sister making self useful by sewing china buttons on papa's dress shirt. Upstairs coolie enjoying florida water. Will probably have to squall to get chow.

May twenty-second

Had exciting time this afternoon, as after mah-jong party everybody went to Chinese theater. Was taken by amah. Had interesting time trying to dodge hot towels thrown from aisles and empty water - melon seeds falling from gallery. Music combination of cook stepping on cat's tail and houseboy breaking dishes. Had seed candy and two peanuts. Had to swallow peanuts all in one piece as found that new teeth don't hit.

Chapter X

In Which the Baby Hears Further Reports of Henli Regatta, Especially About Non-Washable Bathing Suits . . . The Advantages of Bamboo Dragons Over Wooden Elephants . . . Another Encounter with the Jap Baby.

May twenty-third

Nice day, but have funny feeling inside. Auntie busy putting talcum powder on sunburn. Said she saw Bertie at regatta and papa remarked that if he isn't careful they'll cancel his citizenship at the American Consulate for carrying a walking stick more than an inch in diameter.

"I don't know why he didn't row," said Auntie, "He has a wonderful build. I heard that he stands 5 feet 11 inches in his gym suit and weighs 150 pounds in his stocking feet."

Papa said that Bertie was probably like Jess Willard in being a champion heavyweight from the neck down and a champion lightweight from the neck up.

Mama asked papa if he was glad he went to the regatta and he said yes, that he held four aces once and had a full house several times.

"Is that all you got out of it?" asked mama.

"Well," said papa, "I used to wish I could go back for a time and buy a ticket for the Zeigfeld Follies, but after seeing the bathing suits at Henli, I've ceased to be homesick. The tailors who made them must have stolen enough material to buy outfits for the whole family. Most of them were as short as the love letters of a man with a sprained arm."

Auntie said she liked regatta very much, but didn't see why they had people to row when there was a man at the back of the boat to pull it along with strings.

May twenty-fourth

Not much doing today. Sat on floor during tiffin and heard mama ask papa if he would have a mango.

"Do I eat it?" asked papa, "I always

thought the mango was a dance."

"You probably also thought that the papaia was something to play on the ukelele," said mama, with next-door girl expression.

Papa said that he might be ignorant, but at least he didn't tell lady from Japan that he hadn't gone to see the Diabutsu because he didn't like slumming. No answer from mama.

May twenty-fourth, later

Still quiet today. Had pleasant time eating colored spots off bamboo dragon that family bought at Henli. Tried to make it teach wooden elephant how to switch tail, but wooden elephant wouldn't learn. Will take bamboo dragon to Hongkew Park this afternoon and try to throw scare into Jap baby.

May twenty-fifth

Pleasant weather. Missed taking bamboo dragon to Hongkew Park, as papa played with it so much that he broke switch in tail.

Hope he doesn't get interested in my bottle. Would like to keep a few things to myself if possible, as Auntie has taken beauty-pins and amah is using talcum powder for complexion.

May twenty-fifth, later

Mama busy getting ready for bridge party. Was fixing flowers when papa came home to tiffin.

"I've always heard that flowers in China don't smell," said mama, sniffing caterpillar on leaf.

"They're lucky," said papa, "Sometimes I wish I couldn't."

Papa remarked that it was open season for onions on the Whangpoo and that fragrance was strong enough to win all events if only allowed in Far Eastern Olympic.

"The man who named the Garden Bridge must have had a bad cold," said papa.

"Maybe he was thinking of a vegetable garden," mama answered.

Papa said later that national air of China

differed from that of other countries, as other countries expected people to stand up for national air, while that of China knocked people down.

May twenty-fifth

Sat on floor during tiffin, and tried to make friends with wooden elephant again, which was unhappy because of bamboo dragon. Mama said she was busy trying to figure out what to give for bridge prize, as she didn't want to spend money and yet wanted to be sure not to give anything she had won at house of some lady present.

"I think I'll pick out a couple of guest towels without initials," mama said.

"Guest towels were built on the assumption that guests have only half a hand and no face," said papa. "I don't know why a person visiting is supposed to need a towel only one-sixth as big as he uses at home. I always take half a dozen and use them in relays."

Mama said that size of guest towel didn't matter much, as stranger in bathroom always used family towels anyway and merely crumpled up guest towel for form. Manicure amah came just then and mama said she was very glad, as she needed new supply of gossip to entertain company.

May twenty-sixth

Had pleasant ride to Hongkew Park. Saw Jap baby and made face. Jap baby tried to turn up nose at me but couldn't as didn't have enough nose. Had interesting time watching bigger baby take walk in lake with goldfish, while amahs were busy telling about missees' new dresses. Nice day.

May twenty-sixth, later

Came back from ride and found family excited because papa missed light trousers from last year. Mama said we might have key made for wardrobe, but Auntie remarked that would be like locking barn door after stone had stopped gathering moss. Wonder if papa ever saw amah dressed up to visit family.

May twenty-sixth, later

Papa asked mama at tiffin if she had had good time at bridge party, and mama said yes, that she heard three new scandals about ladies' who went to Carlton with people not husband.

"There was some good bridge, too," said mama.

"Not as good as I play," said papa. "Last time I was in a game I made a grand slam by my playing."

"That was a pianola hand," mama answered. "It played itself."

Papa said he didn't get credit for anything except refreshments bought at club, and even there they wouldn't give him beyond the first of the month.

May twenty-seventh

Hongkew Park getting ready for something called Olympics. Wonder if they will enter any Jap babies. Would like to take part in wooden elephant-throwing contest.

May twenty-eighth

Saturday and not much doing. Family went last night to hear lecture on something called relativity. Auntie said she had idea perfectly, only couldn't explain it. Mama remarked that main idea was that everything is sometimes shorter than others, and papa said he was exception to law, as family kept him short all the time.

"When I saw the three balls at the front of the stage I thought the relative was going to be an uncle," papa said.

Mama said she didn't believe so much ether was floating around, as it has an awful smell and everything would seem like hospital.

"Dr. Einstein must have gotten the idea that there is no absolute time by trying to set his watch according to the clocks along Nanking Road," papa said.

Auntie remarked that lecture was just too cute for words but next time she was going to movies.

May twenty-ninth

Pleasant weather. Mama asked papa to go to church in morning and papa said that last time he went, mama took so long to get ready that they missed all the singing and just hit the collection.

"Nobody stylish goes to church on time in Shanghai, and a lot of people just leave cards," said mama. "You needn't worry about the collection either, as all you have to do is sign a chit."

"Yes, but I hate to think of all those chits waiting for me in Heaven and being chased by shroffs with wings," papa answered.

Mama said that if papa really expected to see chits in the Beyond he ought to write them on asbestos. No answer from papa, except prayer about razor.

May twenty-ninth

Spent morning in basement while amah pressed clothes with iron having smokestack in top and told cook's wife about zoo in ancestry. Trouble because cook's wife said amah went to place called Great World with cook. Cook very busy in pantry taking ice out of refrigerator to sell to step-uncle running sherbet stand.

May thirtieth

Rainy day. Papa came back from Hongkew Park and said that baseball game would have been great success if players were only allowed to use sampans. Fat lady called later with other lady just from America who is translating Chinese poems into English.

"You learned Chinese pretty quickly," said papa.

"Oh, I don't know any Chinese, said lady, swinging brown glass beads, "I just translate."

"I'm familiar with that type of work, as I've done a little of it myself," said papa. "Here is a fragment I translated from Li Po: 'Oh laundryman, spreading wash in Hongkew, How the morning sun shines on sheets and pillow-cases! Are you thinking of Confucius as you stand in the sun-light, Or are you merely wondering if family will miss those silk pajamas?'"

Poetry lady said poem was very unusual, and papa said it was not easy to write, as he had lots of trouble getting poetic license from Municipal Council. Papa then asked if he should recite another poem, but lady said she guessed she'd better be going.

May thirty-first

Quiet day. Mama told papa he ought to improve mind by going to meeting of Shanghai Psychic Research Society.

"It's all about spirits," said mama.

"Will they teach me how to make home-brew in case I go back to the States?" asked papa.

Mama said it was not that kind of spirits, but the kind you see through.

Papa answered that in that case he didn't want to go, as he could do research work enough sitting in lobby of Palace Hotel and watching summer girls come in door.

Chapter XI

In Which the Baby Has a Brief Glimpse of the Far Eastern Olympics . . . Economical Phases of the Dinner Dance . . . The Battle of the Sukiaki House . . . The Mosquito Massage as an Indoor Sport.

June first

Nice morning. Sat on floor upstairs and watched coolie put up netting to keep mosquitoes from getting away from bed. Papa came home from Hongkew Park and said he hadn't seen so many kimonos outdoors since big hotel burned down in America.

"Was the track meet any good?" asked mama.

"Yes," answered papa, "but I know a ricsha coolie that could beat any of them. The only trouble is that they wouldn't let him enter his ricsha and he wouldn't know how to run without it."

Mama said track-meet might be pretty good, but that she could see a better one by standing at corner of Nanking and Szechuen Roads and watching people cross street at noon-time.

June second
Not much doing today. Went to Hongkew Park, but Sikh policeman said perambulator and its chauffeur would have to stay outside grounds. Heard noise inside like orphan asylum calling for bottle. Must have been chorus of Jap babies.

June third
Nice day. Lady who is house-hunting called at tiffin and mama asked her if she had found any place.

"Yes," said lady. "We have the choice of sharing an attic room with two poodles or renting apartment for summer, provided we take over furniture and husband."

Mama told papa that family landlord had called and asked for two hundred taels a month, but papa said to tell him that he was no Rudyard Kipling and couldn't think up that many.

June fourth

Rain. Auntie excited about man who had invited her to party at Carlton.

"His friends are very prominent," said Auntie, trying yellow georgette against sunburn.

"So are his ears," said papa, looking up from pink sheet.

Auntie didn't say anything then, but remarked later that the only trouble with dancing at Carlton was that nobody kept in step because they were all busy trying to see who everybody else was with.

June sixth

Not much doing today. Boy busy putting mothballs in pockets of papa's winter suits and taking out change. Nothing left but coppers, as mama had been there first. Papa said at tiffin that moth-balls might keep moths away from clothes, but they also keep everybody else away after suits were resurrected in the fall. Also that for weeks afterwards, he found himself giving moth-balls for fare in tram. Hope they don't put my wooden elephant in moth-balls, as may cut more teeth during summer.

June sixth, later

Mama told papa that family had invitation to dinner dance for end of the week. Papa said dinner dance was great economy, as boy always put down soup or other course just before music began and then took it away during dance, before anybody had chance to damage it. Mama told him he shouldn't try to sit out, as every time he did it, it meant that lady had to sit out too, but papa replied that he was going to step on all ladies' toes early in evening so that they would be glad to let him eat dinner.

June seventh

Nice day. Went for ride to Hongkew Park and saw Jap baby in front of sukiyaki house kept by Jap papa. Pointed at Jap baby with chin like houseboy and then made face. Baby squalled and Jap papa came out of next-door shop where he was having shoes half-soled by carpenter. Wiped Jap baby's nose with Japanese poem on towel. Didn't see me, as amah had sighted another Chinese lady who didn't know story of foreign lady's new third husband and had put perambulator in high.

June eighth

Weather still good. Mama asked Auntie if she had good time at cafe last night in new dress that tailor had copied from window on Nanking Road. Auntie said she would have had better time if seven other ladies had not also copied dress, but that anyway she had enjoyed seeing next door girl sit out dances and had also noticed five ladies dancing with their own husbands. Papa said maybe next door girl had something wrong with foot, but Auntie remarked that it was probably because she is pigeon-toed in features.

June ninth

Weather pretty good. Mama told papa that, if he doesn't screen lower part of house pretty soon, she will have to eat dinner with feet in pillow-case.

"If you would only eat dinner with your head in a pillow-case, I'd have more quiet in which to enjoy food," papa said.

Mama remarked that when he enjoyed food, nobody else had any quiet, didn't hear more as amah came in just then to give me bath with laundry soap.

June tenth

Nice day. Auntie very excited. Said Bertie had almost proposed to her at Carlton, but was interrupted by having to go across room to see friend.

"He has a regular path worn around the Carlton from getting up to see friends when the Chinese boy brings in the arithmetic," said papa.

Auntie said papa didn't seem to know that Bertie was valuable office man and that he is an expert on the touch system.

"I'll say he is," said papa, "He touched me for ten dollars once and it's still absent."

Mama said she loved romance and asked Auntie what Bertie had said.

"He told me that he would cling to me as

UNEXPURGATED DIARY OF A SHANGHAI BABY

long as a ricsha coolie does to a straw hat." said Auntie clasping hands and looking at fly on ceiling.

Papa said that if Auntie wanted to be certain, she would make Bertie promise to cling to her as long as he does to five dollar bill.

June eleventh

Rain. Sat on floor while papa dug dark clothes out of trunk and said things as he threw moth-balls from pockets. Was put in crib later for nap and watched massage amah look through wardrobe while mama's face was under hot towel. Later had interesting time downstairs as coolie beat carpets with papa's golf-clubs. Might borrow golf club some day to try on Jap baby. Hope Jap papa won't object.

June twelfth

Rain. Family sat in parlor during morning, after papa said he didn't want to go out, as was afraid of growing fins.

"The only time you ever went to church

without being driven was when we were married," said mama.

"Yes, and look what happened to me then," papa answered. Squalled then on account of having sat on price tag with stickers, which Auntie had thrown on floor, so mama called amah to give me chow.

June twelfth, later

Sat with family again in parlor after nap. Auntie busy with snapshots taken on houseboat trip, pasting them in album. Said she didn't know whether or not to put in one of girls wading, as her features didn't show up very good.

"Don't worry about that," said papa, picking up snapshot. "Nobody will waste any time looking at your features."

Auntie told papa that she never did take a very good picture in the sunlight.

"The only way you could ever take a good picture would be to go into the Louvre and walk off with Mona Lisa or something," papa said.

No answer from Auntie, who was busy

pasting in view of men and girls who had changed hats.

June thirteenth

More rain. Went out for little while in afternoon when shower stopped but didn't have very good time, as amah stopped perambulator with back wheels on street and rest on sidewalk while she had long talk with Chinese lady. Wonder if she thinks my neck is made out of India rubber. Tried to tell mama when I came back, but mama said, "Yes, darling. Daddy will be home pretty soon."

Family as dense as crowd at Far Eastern Olympic.

June fourteenth

Family excited because of red spots on my face. Mama said I was getting measles. Nobody seemed to notice that Auntie had looped back mosquito net on crib with ribbon so as to make room look better when girl friends called. Squalled last night, but family didn't tumble. Jiggled wooden elephant in front of me to keep me quiet. Wonder what will happen tonight.

June fifteenth

All rest of family have same kind of measles. Papa asked Auntie what she was lighting when he came home from office.

"It's punk," said auntie, lighting another stick.

"I'll tell the world it is," said papa, sniffing air. "Why don't you put it out?"

Auntie said purpose was to knock out mosquitoes under table and papa remarked that if it burned very long, mosquitoes under table would have to move over and make room for him.

"For the next few months, all Shanghai girls will walk like a fly wiping its feet after stepping on mucilage," papa said. "Anybody who wants to make himself popular ought to get up a dance with that stop in it."

Mama said custom of withdrawing after dinner at parties was very convenient in summer, as it gave ladies chance to massage bites.

UNEXPURGATED DIARY OF A SHANGHAI BABY

Chapter XII

In Which the Baby is introduced to the Fly Season . . . The Clothes Soviet in Shanghai . . . Papa Plays With Funny Round Things at Party . . . The Baby Just Misses Being Handed Over to Amateurs.

JUNE sixteenth

Still raining. Auntie worried because Bertie was likely to be sent home on business trip.

"You have a right to worry," said papa. "The hardest working vamps in the world are the ones on the Pacific steamers. They can steal any man on the boat not under lock and key. If Cleopatra crossed with Mark Anthony, she'd probably have to spend her evenings in the salon playing dominoes with a missionary, while Mark held down the deck with some blond going to Manila."

Mama said it was too bad some company didn't insure girls against loss of beaus who crossed ocean, but papa said there wouldn't be any money in it for firm, as risks were too great.

"How do you happen to know all this?" mama asked, with squint in eye, but papa said he had to be back to office early.

June seventeenth

Weather very hot. Wish they would dress me with apron in front and string in back like Chinese babies, or in georgette shoulder straps like mama. Mama asked papa why he wore dark suit on warm day.

"Because I don't want to be arrested," said papa, "I've got a suit for every day in the week and this is it."

Mama asked papa where all his summer clothes are, and papa said that some are with the amah and some are with the houseboy. Remarked later that he was sorry he had bought transparent raincoat, as chief job of raincoat is to cover up old clothes, but transparent ones spotted bluff.

June eighteenth

More rain. Hope it stops before Hongkew

UNEXPURGATED DIARY OF A SHANGHAI BABY

Park is washed away as have few more remarks to make to Jap baby.

June nineteenth

Weather warm. Sat on floor in kitchen and watched coolie catch flies to put in new flytrap. When trap was crowded, coolie emptied it out of open window. Flies must have liked trap as all came back. Flies also very fond of rubber on my bottle, but don't mind very much as amah always scares them away before giving it to me. Have swallowed only one so far. Heard mama tell Auntie that papa is too fly, and Auntie said yes, that he is always buzzing around. Wonder if he knows about trap.

June twentieth

Rain. Mama told papa she had been reading in paper about cutting trees down in Public Gardens.

'The baby spends so much time down there that he will miss them a lot," said mama.

"Why?" asked papa, "Does the amah

climb trees with him?"

Mama told papa not to be any more foolish than he is naturally and said that everybody would miss the beautiful limbs.

"Oh, I don't know," said papa. "Just take a walk down the Bund during the typhoon season and you'll see more limbs than you can count."

Mama told papa that she thought he had better come up to Tsingtao for August.

June twenty-first

Weather a little better. Auntie busy pulling out eye-brows and making new ones with pencil. Said she didn't know what she would do about complexion in the hot weather, as powder always looked like wet flour and melted color showed so badly on shoulders of monkey-jackets.

"I don't worry any about my complexion and lots of people are wild about me," papa said.

"You mean that lots of the people about you are wild," mama answered.

Papa said that anyway his friends didn't

spend all afternoon over cup of tea and two macaroons wondering how lady next door could afford sequin gown when husband was only Number 4 in office.

June twenty-second

Not much doing today. Went calling with amah in house with Chinese baby. Amah gave the baby my bottle to try, but baby didn't like it. Then amah passed it to baby's sisters and brothers. Squalled, as thought I might need drink on the way home. Amah filled up rest of bottle with tea. Better than rubber mouthpiece with no connection, but not as good as regular chow.

June twenty-fourth

Friday. Papa busy looking over clothes brought by washmen.

"He must have a new customer," said papa. "Here is a shirt I never saw before."

Papa said that laundered clothes in Shanghai are owned on a community basis and everybody wears them in turn.

"I saw one of my shirts on a Bubbling

Well car today and another one almost ran over me on a motor-cycle," papa remarked.

Glad my clothes are washed by amah, as would hate laundry to deal me Jap baby's kimono.

June twenty-fifth

Interesting time. Papa came home with friends after mama went out to tea-party. Friends asked if mama was likely to come back soon, and papa said no, not if she once gets to talking, and that coast was as clear as at American Club.

"Put a little snow on Fuji," said friend twirling round white thing into center of green cloth. Lots more talk I didn't understand. Heard papa say later that he was going to put Auntie on the table, but didn't know how he could as she was still at tea-party.

June twenty-fifth, later

Crawled under couch and went to sleep, but woke up when boy said missee was coming. Somebody threw round things down under couch cover and somebody else pushed in bottles.

"We've been talking over some business," said papa, as mama came in.

Thought I would surprise mama. Crawled out with red round thing in my hand to give her but knocked over bottle while getting out.

"We've just had tea," said papa, looking nervous.

"I never heard it called that before," said mama, picking up bottle and reading label.

Papa's friends said they would have to go on account of important date and papa remarked that he would see them to ricshas. Ricshas must have been a long way off, as papa is still out.

EPILOGUE

July third

Great excitement. Family going back to America. Papa says mama will have lovely time breaking in Swede servant girl if any, and that she had better ask amah to draw diagram of safety-pins in my attire. Auntie busy buying clothes for shipboard but papa said that if she is still as good a sailor as she was coming over, all she needs is nightdress.

Squalled all day, as hate idea of being dressed and brought up by amateurs. Heard mama say she was going to give goldfish to amah. Wish I was a goldfish.

July fifth

Family still busy packing. Auntie says Bertie has asked her to stay, but she says she will look at crowd on boat before deciding. Papa packing clothes in bird-cage, as mama has taken up all room in trunk.

July seventh
Family leaving. Tried to hide in closet, so as to be forgotten, but mama found me when looking for lost handbag. Still squalling about losing amah.

July seventh
Final bulletin - Great surprise. Amah coming with us. Passed Jap baby on way, to steamer and threw chow bottle. Very happy. Wonder if being baby in America is any easier than in Shanghai.

GLOSSARY

Houseboy - The major factotum in a Far Eastern household. He waits on table, answers the doorbell and telephone, and usually directs the other servants.

Coolie - A servant of lower rank who usually does ninety per cent of the work. The term is also applied to all unskilled laborers in China.

Tiffin - The meal which at home is known as lunch or luncheon, depending on whether or not there are flowers on the table.

Chow - Anything to eat.

Carlton - One of Shanghai's most popular dancing resorts.

Bund - The street skirting Shanghai's waterfront, on the Whangpoo River.

Shroff - A Chinese bill-collector employed by local firms to present signed chits on the first of every month and secure payment if possible. Very unpopular among foreigners.

Amah - The lady servant who guides the destinies of foreign children in China. She is also the unprinted newspaper that keeps local gossip in circulation.

Chit - A bill signed in restaurants, cafes, or stores as a promise to pay; also a note carried by a coolie. The large number of coolies and the eccentricities of the telephone system make the chit a very popular method of communication.

Taipan - The manager of a firm or office. The social system in the East gives the taipan a large amount of prestige, regardless of his drawing-room qualifications.